In the fairytale treasury which has come into the world's common possession, there is no doubt that Hans Christian Andersen's stories are of outstanding character. Their symbolism is loaded with Christian values, and some of them are direct illustrations of the gospel. From his early childhood in the town of Odense, Denmark, until his death in Copenhagen, Hans Christian Andersen (1805-1875) had a valid Christian faith which came to expression in many of the approximately 150 stories and tales he wrote. In one of them, he states: "In every human life, whether poor or great, there is an invisible thread that shows we belong to God." The thread in Andersen's stories is one of optimism which has given hope and inspiration to people all over the world.

It is in this spirit the Scandinavia Fairy Tales is published. We are convinced of the validity of teaching spiritual principles and building character values through imaginative stories, just as Jesus used parables to teach the people of his time.

THE LITTLE MATCH GIRL
By Hans Christian Andersen
Translated from the original Danish text by Marlee Alex
Illustrated by Toril Marö Henrichsen
Published by Scandinavia Publishing House,
Nørregade 32, DK-1165 Copenhagen; Denmark
Text:© Copyright 1984 Scandinavia Publishing House
Artwork:© Copyright 1984 Toril Marö Henrichsen and
Scandinavia Publishing House
Printed in Italy

ISBN 87 87732 55 6

The Little Match Girl

Hans Christian Andersen
Translated from the original Danish text
by Marlee Alex
Illustrated by Toril Marö Henrichsen
Scandinavia Publishing House

It was terribly cold. It was snowing and began to get dark as evening approached. It was the last evening of the year, New Year's Eve. In this cold and in this darkness, a little girl walked along the street; a poor girl with a bare head and bare feet. She had slippers on when she left home, but what did that help? They were big slippers which her mother had last used. They were so big that the little girl lost them as she hurried over the street to avoid being hit by two racing carriages. She could not find one of the slippers, and a boy ran off with the other one. He said he could use it as a cradle when he himself had children.

The little girl's small feet were red and blue from the cold. In an old apron she carried some matchsticks and in her hand she held another bundle of them. No one had bought from her that day, no one had given her a penny. She was hungry, freezing and dejected looking; the poor little thing!

Snowflakes fell in her long, golden hair which curled so beautifully around her shoulders. But she wasn't thinking about how she looked. In all the windows candles were shining, and even in the street it smelled wonderfully of roast goose! It was New Year's Eve! That's what she was thinking about.

In a corner between two houses, one of which stuck out into the street further than the other, she sat down and huddled up. She drew her small legs up under her but she grew even colder. And she dared not go home again for she hadn't sold any of the matchsticks; she hadn't earned a single penny. Her father would beat her. And besides, it was just as cold at home. They had only a poor roof over their heads through which the wind blew, though the biggest cracks were stuffed with straw and rags.

Her small hands were
almost completely numb with the cold.
Oh! A little matchstick might help, if only
she dared to pull one out of the bundle, strike it against
the wall and warm her fingers. She drew one out, »ritsch!«. How
it sputtered, how it flickered! It was warm and bright like
a little candle. When she held her hand around
it, it gave a strange light.

It seemed to the little girl as if she was sitting before a large iron stove with shiny brass knobs and brass handles. The fire blazed gloriously. It warmed her so nicely. But, what was this? The little girl stretched out her feet to warm them as well, and the flame went out. The stove disappeared. She sat with the stub of the burned out match in her hand.

She struck a new one; it flickered, it flared
up, and where it shone on the wall, the wall
became transparent as a veil. She saw
right into a parlor where the table was set
with a shiny white cloth and fine
dinnerware. Steam from the roast goose,
stuffed with prunes and apples, rose into
the air. And what was even more
remarkable, the goose jumped down from
the platter, and waddled across the floor
with a fork and a knife in its back. Right
over to the poor little girl, it came; then the
flame went out and there was only the
thick, cold wall to see.

She struck another match,
and found herself sitting under the
loveliest Christmas tree. It was
larger and prettier
than the one she had seen through the
glass-door of the rich merchant.
A thousand candles flickered
on the green branches, and colored
pictures like the ones decorating the store
windows, looked down at her.
The little girl reached out toward the tree,
and the match went out.
The many candles rose higher
and higher into the sky. She saw now
that they were bright starts. One of them
fell and drew a long stripe of
fire across the sky.

"Someone is dying now!
" said the little girl. Her old
Grandmother, the only
person who had been good to
her but who was now dead,
had said: when a star fell, a
soul went up to God.
She struck another
matchstick against the wall. It
shone around her, and in the
glimmer stood the old
woman; her Grandmother, so
bright, looking radient and bright,
gentle and loving.

"Grandma!" shouted the little girl, "Oh, take me with you! I know you will disappear when the match goes out; disappear just like the stove, the lovely goose, and the big, wonderful Christmas tree! And she quickly struck the remnant of the matchsticks in the bundle, for she wanted to keep Grandmother within reach. The matches lit up with such a glow that they were brighter than daylight. Grandmother had never before been so beautiful, so strong; she lifted the little girl up in her arms, and they flew in glory and joy, so high, so high. And there was no cold, no hunger, no fear. They were with God.

20

But in the cold morning,
the little girl sat in the
corner by the house, with rosy
cheeks and a smile on her
lips, dead; frozen to death
the last evening of the old year.
New Year's morn rose over the little
body which was found
with the burnt out matchsticks.
People said she had tried to warm
herself. None of them knew what beautiful
things she had seen,
nor how, with her old Grandmother,
she had gloriously entered into
the New Year's joy.

Explaining the story:

This is a story about needs. We all have needs, and we all have dreams or ideas about how those needs should be met, and what will really make us happy. However, the satisfaction of our physical needs will only last a short time, and we will find ourselves unhappy again. Real happiness comes through seeking God and having a relationship with Him.

Talking about the truth of the story:

The little match girl is an example of what is poor, helpless, and hungry within each one of us. The world may be insensitive to our needs but God sees them and He will fully satisfy them. See Matthew 5:3-8.

1. Why did the little girl sit down all alone in the cold city?
2. The flickering matches revealed her four primary needs.
What were these needs?
3. How did each one bring her closer to God?

Applying the truth of the story:

1. Can you think of some ways in which your needs bring you closer to God?
2. The people on the street passed by the little match girl; can you think of some ways you can reach out to meet the needs of others?